How the
Rhinoceros
Got His Skin

Retold by Elizabeth Rogers

Illustrated by Tomislav Zlatic

FRANKLIN WATTS
LONDON•SYDNEY

First published in 2010 by
Franklin Watts
338 Euston Road
London
NW1 3BH

Franklin Watts Australia
Level 17/207 Kent Street
Sydney
NSW 2000

A CIP catalogue record for this book is available
from the British Library.

ISBN 978 0 7496 9406 7 (hbk)
ISBN 978 0 7496 9412 8 (pbk)

Series Editor: Jackie Hamley
Series Advisor: Catherine Glavina
Series Designer: Peter Scoulding

Printed in China

Franklin Watts is a division of
Hachette Children's Books,
an Hachette UK company.
www.hachette.co.uk

This Just So story is
based on a tale written
by an author called
Rudyard Kipling over
a hundred years ago.

Just So stories give fun
ideas for why different
animals are like they are.

One day, a man made a cake.

4

Rhinoceros smelt it,
and charged over.

He ate up all the
man's cake.

6

Big mistake!

7

That summer,
Rhinoceros came
to swim.

In those days, his
smooth skin had buttons
so he could take it off.

Rhinoceros took off his skin, and left it on the shore.

The man took the skin.

The man filled the skin
with cake crumbs ...

... and then put it back.

When Rhinoceros put
on his skin, it itched.

Rhinoceros scratched until he rubbed off the buttons and made his skin wrinkly.

Rhinoceros could never
get the crumbs out.

And that's how he got
such wrinkly skin!

Puzzle Time!

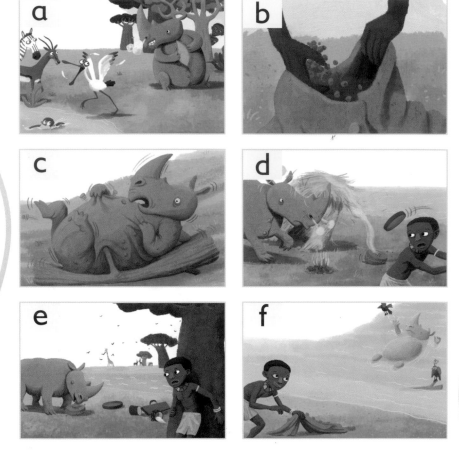

Put these pictures in the right order and tell the story!

annoyed

greedy

fed up

rude

Which words describe Rhinoceros
and which describe the man?

Turn over for answers!

Notes for adults

TADPOLES are structured to provide support for newly independent readers. The stories may also be used by adults for sharing with young children.

Starting to read alone can be daunting. **TADPOLES** help by providing visual support and repeating words and phrases. These books will both develop confidence and encourage reading and rereading for pleasure.

If you are reading this book with a child, here are a few suggestions:

1. Make reading fun! Choose a time to read when you and the child are relaxed and have time to share the story.

2. Talk about the story before you start reading. Look at the cover and the blurb. What might the story be about? Why might the child like it?

3. Encourage the child to retell the story, using the jumbled picture puzzle as a starting point. Extend vocabulary with the matching words to characters puzzle.

4. Talk about how the story has fun with how different animals look, and see if you can think of other animals and why they might look the way they do.

5. Give praise! Remember that small mistakes need not always be corrected.

Answers

Here is the correct order:

1. d 2. e 3. a 4. f 5. b 6. c

Words to describe
Rhinoceros:
greedy, rude

Words to describe the man:
annoyed, fed up